Sally the Apple Tree Makes a New Friend

ISBN 978-1-0980-3680-5 (paperback)
ISBN 978-1-0980-3681-2 (digital)

Christian Faith Publishing, Inc.
832 Park Avenue
Meadville, PA 16335
www.christianfaithpublishing.com

Printed in the United States of America

Sally the Apple Tree Makes a New Friend

Lori Nottingham

Illustrated by Freida Nottingham

Sally the Apple Tree had been sleeping all winter long until spring came. It was time for her to wake up. She stretched her branches and opened her eyes. As she looked around, she saw children playing everywhere, except one child who was all alone, leaning against her trunk. Sally bent down and asked the little girl her name. She mumbled something that sounded like Sarah.

Sarah had a long and sad face.

Sally asked, “Why are you so sad?”

Sarah replied, "I just moved here. I miss my old school and all of my friends."

Sally lovingly lowered a branch, gently patted Sarah on her head, and said, "I'll be your friend! Would you like to swing on my branches?"

Sarah nodded her head up and down, as to say yes.

Sally, in a friendly manner, lowered two long branches and made a seat for Sarah to swing on.

Amazingly, Sarah was able to sit and smile while Sally gently swayed her branches back and forth. Sally asked Sarah to tell her about her old school and friends. Sarah talked about her three friends Morgan, Amber, and Clare. She told the apple tree how they used to play Barbie dolls and sometimes tag. Sarah said she and her friends would sometimes argue and that they learned how to work out their problems. She talked about her teacher, Mrs. Stewart and the many stories she would read to her class.

Sally asked, “Well, have you tried to make new friends?”

Sarah answered, “No. I don’t think anyone wants to be my friend. They already have their friends. They don’t need a new friend.”

“What do you think you and your friends would have done if there were a new student at your school?” inquired Sally.

Sarah chuckled as she thought about how she and her friends enjoyed making new friends. She went on to say, “We would proudly show them around our school and have them play with us. We would introduce them to everyone at school, show them where the bathrooms were, and the red line we couldn’t cross during recess. It was fun showing them where everything was.”

In a soft voice, Sally asked Sarah, “Have you given your new classmates a chance to get to know you?”

"What do you mean?" replied Sarah.

"Has your teacher introduced you to your new classmates and asked them to help you find your way around the school?" asked Sally.

"Why, yes, she did." Sarah stopped swinging for a moment. She paused to think about what she was going to say. "You know, Sally, I need to give my classmates a chance to get to know me. When I get back to class, I'm going to let them get to know me and try not to act so shy. Thanks so much, Sally, for being my friend. I better get in line before my teacher comes. Thanks again!"

The next day, Sally eagerly waited to see Sarah. Sarah did not come to Sally the Apple Tree. Sally saw her playing dodgeball with a whole group of children. Sarah stopped and looked Sally's way. She waved to Sally and pointed to her new friends. Sally smiled and waved a long branch back. Sally was very pleased with her new friend.

The original Sally the Apple Tree drawn by Sarah Nottingham age 6

About the Author

Lori Nottingham is long-time educator. She is married with three grown children and one grandson. She lives in the beautiful state of Arizona. Her hobbies all have to do with nature. She enjoys hiking, camping, and gardening. Her motto in life is, "The more you practice at something, the better you get." Persevere through the hard tasks.

About the Illustrator

Freida Nottingham started drawing at a young age. She then began painting as a teenager. She uses all mediums, including murals in her church. She then put her talent in thread. She is known as the "Artist in Thread." She has inspired her grandchildren in art as well. At the age of 88, she continues her passion. "It's a great way to express yourself!"

CPSIA information can be obtained
at www.ICGtesting.com
Printed in the USA
LVHW011425111220
673921LV00005B/177